MY RED VELVET CAPE

Sleeping Bear Press™

2395 South Huron Parkway, Suite 200
Ann Arbor, MI 48104
www.sleepingbearpress.com

Printed and bound in the United States.

10 9 8 7 6 5 4 3 2 1

Library of Congress Cataloging-in-Publication Data

Names: Sullivan, Dana, author, illustrator.
Title: My red velvet cape / written and illustrated by Dana Sullivan.
Description: Ann Arbor, MI : Sleeping Bear Press, [2018] | Summary: Mateo
imagines amazing things he might do with the cape his grandmother is bringing
for his birthday, until his sister informs him it will be a cake, instead.
Identifiers: LCCN 2017029810 | ISBN 9781585363933
Subjects: | CYAC: Birthdays—Fiction. | Gifts—Fiction. | Cloaks—
Fiction. | Grandmothers—Fiction. | Hispanic Americans—Fiction.
Classification: LCC PZ7.S95137 My 2018 | DDC [E]—dc23
LC record available at https://lccn.loc.gov/2017029810

To my faithful sidekick, Bennie

—DS

"Grandma made me a **red velvet cape** for my birthday! I can't wait for my superhero party today!"

"It's time to get ready for my costume party. Lots of friends are coming!"

"Welcome, everybody! Just wait 'til my grandma gets here. She's bringing my **red velvet cape!**"

"It's your birthday. She's bringing you a **red velvet CAKE!**"

"Mateo! Look what Grandma brought you!"

"Thank you for the cake, Grandma."

"Oh no! I didn't know you wanted a **CAKE**! I'm so sorry. I made you a . . ."

"red velvet

CAPE!"